FANTASTICAL CHRISTMAS VOLUME 1

CONNOR WHITELEY

No part of this book may be reproduced in any form or by any electronic or mechanical means. Including information storage, and retrieval systems, without written permission from the author except for the use of brief quotations in a book review.

This book is NOT legal, professional, medical, financial or any type of official advice.

Any questions about the book, rights licensing, or to contact the author, please email connorwhiteley@connorwhiteley.net

Copyright © 2023 CONNOR WHITELEY

All rights reserved.

DEDICATION
Thank you to all my readers without you I couldn't do what I love.

AUTHOR OF THE FIREHEART FANTASY SERIES

CONNOR WHITELEY

MAGIC THAT BINDS

A HOLIDAY CONTEMPORARY FANTASY SHORT STORY

MAGIC THAT BINDS

It might have started off as a hobby but to Janet making gifts was all part of the holiday season experience. It was amazing, wonderful to make people such wondrous gifts, Janet was known to everyone in Kent, England as the best gift maker because of her ability to infuse even the most hideous objects with her magic and make them stunning.

Janet stood in a smaller isle in a massive craft superstore surrounded by rows upon rows of beads in all their different sizes, textures and colours.

Beads might have been awful, small and annoying to some people, but to Janet they were magical things that were the best material to make gifts from. Their small round size meant it didn't take much magic to manipulate them into whatever shape she wanted.

And as a part-time teacher at the local sixth form for young magic users, the beads were perfect to allow them to experiment with their magic.

She had stopped using wooden and other large material a long time ago, young inexperienced magic users definitely shouldn't unleash the magical energy needed to manipulate large pieces of wood until they were ready.

Janet hated to think about all the fires, explosions and other accidents caused by them.

But beads were perfect.

The smell of the little plastic beads wasn't the best but when mixed together with flowers, natural materials and maybe even a hint of lavender, these beads would smell amazing, and that was what Janet loved about gift making.

The sound of other customers and their children in the other isles reminded Janet of her own love of the different crafts. She loved the bright lively strokes of painting and the wonderful hands-on nature of pottery.

But the containers of bright red, blue and green beads in front of her head were what Janet needed at this point in time. Maybe she could check out the paints and pottery bits later. Perhaps even her husband could buy her a few pieces for Christmas.

Janet placed her hands into the containers of the plastic beads. Their icy coldness felt amazing, their smooth cold texture was a stunning, beautiful contrast to her aged rough hands.

But she needed to find magic sensitive beads.

These types of beads were often made by magic users in the factories and mixed in with the rest of the beads to stop them from being detected (Not everyone was as respectable towards magic users as they should have been), but Janet had detected a strong number of the magical beads in this aisle alone.

That was unusual yet that was the last thing on Janet's priorities at the moment as her annoying (but wonderfully rich) client had given her an awful deadline to make a gift by the end of the day.

Janet didn't like to rush gifts. Each one was carefully planned, made and delivered. Each one took at least three days to make so making a wonderful gift in a single day was going to be difficult. Not impossible. Just difficult.

The only solace Janet could take from the impossible request was the amazing contract and payday that came with it. Ten thousand pounds for the gift and the exclusive contract of being the client's personal gift maker.

Normally that wouldn't interest Janet, but considering the client was a rich businessman who entertained hundreds of clients every year in London. The pay checks would be like shooting fish in a barrel.

Janet finished searching the containers in front of her head and frowned.

This was silly. She had detected the magic here and now they were gone. She was running out of time. Janet had to create this gift in time.

Janet closed her eyes and called on her powers, she used them to sense and search through the containers, if the beads were here then her magic should be able to find them.

Nothing. Except the moderately strong remains of their magical signatures.

Janet hated that the beads had been so close but she was too late to get them. Perhaps she could go and search the store and maybe the car park, then buy them off the person who had them, but Janet wasn't sure in the slightest.

"Mrs Janet Oblong?" an elderly lady said.

Janet looked at the tall elderly lady with her purple power suit, long brown hair and perfectly aged face. Janet couldn't understand how the woman could sound like a ninety-year-old but look not a day over thirty.

Well, she could. The woman had to be a fellow magic user.

"How do you know my name?" Janet asked.

The woman smiled. "I am Lady Michelle, and I know a lot about you,"

Janet didn't believe her in the slightest.

"Janet Oblong grew up in Canterbury England and went to university at The University of Magic in the city for five years, completing a degree in Psychology specialising in Magical Mental Health and then doing another degree in Magical Studies,"

Janet was impressed but surely this woman could have found all that out online. Maybe this Lady was a creepy stalker or something.

"I'm not a stalker, Janet,"

Janet's eyes widened.

"And before you think it, I am a telepath. That is my main discipline. My husband Lord Michelle is a lot better at it but I manage,"

Janet wanted to wonder who the hell this woman was, but she didn't, she couldn't have this Lady Michelle reading her thoughts. So she fell back on her training and what her degree had taught her to do.

Simply don't think about anything important.

"Clever Janet. I wasn't sure if you remembered your training,"

Janet stepped forward. "Do I know you?"

"In a way. I always watched your classes. Loved University myself. But I was always at the edges of everyone's mind,"

Janet took a step back. "Who the hell are you?"

"You seek beads to make a gift. I have beads and want a gift,"

Janet didn't even care if the woman read her mind anymore. This was just strange and crazy, the Lady Michelle was clearly a stalker of some kind. It wasn't natural for a telepath or any magic user to watch university students and read the thoughts at the edge of their minds.

It was probably the weirdest thing Janet had ever heard of.

"Oh now Janet, I have heard of stranger things. Me brushing past the edges of your mind isn't strange. It's comforting. I'm a guardian of sorts,"

Janet just wanted those beads and to go home.

She didn't have time for this Lady Michelle, or whatever the hell she was.

"A Guardian?" Janet asked, her voice unsure.

"Yes dear Janet. I used to work for the University's Mental Health Services and I spent my day brushing through the minds of the students checking on their wellbeing,"

"You're lying. You didn't check on their wellbeing. You invaded their privacy, and doesn't magical law prohibit you searching the minds of others?"

Lady Michelle laughed hard. "Dearest Janet, the Law is old and outdated. I might have scarred myself by looking through the thoughts of the students, and believe me it's... interesting what some people get up to. But I saved lives,"

Janet realised this woman certainly wasn't normal, but she felt like a woman with a purpose. This was no chance meeting or simply seeing Janet and wanting to talk. Lady Michelle had planned to meet her and make Janet talk to her.

"My client's your husband, isn't he?" Janet asked.

Lady Michelle nodded. "Clever girl. Sure, my husband doesn't know I am here but still. He wants the gift for me and I want something from you in return,"

"What?" Janet asked, checking for the nearest escape route.

"I want you to work for me,"

Janet's eyes narrowed. "Work for you? I don't

even know what you do,"

A family of small children and two parents walked into the aisle and Lady Michelle gestured Janet to walk with her.

It was hard to keep up with Lady Michelle's long legs but Janet managed.

"Me and my Husband might be members of the English Nobility but we have a side business too,"

Whatever it was Janet didn't want any part in it. From her years of experience, all side businesses were criminal and dodgy as any criminal gang. Hell, most the side businesses Janet had dealt with were ran by criminals.

She had to get the beads and escape.

"We are not criminals Janet,"

Damn! Janet had forgotten about the telepath thing. She had to remain focused and forget her thoughts.

"What is this side business?" Janet asked.

Lady Michelle looked around. "Coast is clear. You know the Anti-Supernatural Bill going through the Houses of Parliament and Lords at the moment,"

Janet couldn't believe she would even mention such an outrageous thing in a public place. The Bill, Act or whatever else the UK government decided to call it would ruin her and her business.

All Janet wanted was to make jewellery, sell it and give people joy in their lives. She wasn't going to hurt anyone, but just because a gang of five magic users decided to go round killing people, the UK

Government saw its chance to make magic illegal.

It was wrong!

Janet had wanted to move to Scotland more times than she cared to admit because their leaders seemed to like Magic Users. But it didn't matter in the end, if the UK Government made magic illegal then it would find a way to make Scotland make it illegal too.

The wonders of UK politics!

Janet frowned. "What about it?"

Lady Michelle looked around again. "Me and my husband are the only Magic Users in UK politics. The Bill will pass and our people will be doomed,"

Janet wanted to leave now. It would be Christmas in a few weeks, all she wanted to do was make her gifts and get on with her life. She didn't want to think about this.

"The Bill will be passed before Christmas," Lady Michelle said.

"Why tell me this? I am a simple Gift Maker,"

Lady Michelle smiled. "That is why I sought you out. Ever since I first met... brush your mind at university I knew you were different. You love the world, you love magic, you love your creations. I do not believe you want that to end on your watch,"

Janet hated when other people were right. Especially this Lady Michelle, Janet loved creating gifts, spreading the joy and showing others the wonders of magic. She didn't want to stop, she wasn't going to stop, no matter what the Law was.

Lady Michelle knelt in front of Janet. "I am

begging you Janet Oblong to help me,"

The sight of a Lady kneeling on the ground and getting dust and dirt all over her power suit was something, and Janet realised that these words weren't the act of a malice or manipulative woman.

These were the words of a scared woman who just wanted to do the best for her people.

"Rise Lady Michelle," Janet said, always wanting to say that. "What must I do?"

Lady Michelle got the beads out of her pocket.

"I need you to make a gift. I need you to make a gift that is so great for all 600 members of Parliament. Show the Elected Officials of the UK what magic can offer. Prove to them the power of magic and how joyous it is and show them how magic binds us all together,"

"What about the Lords?" Janet asked.

Lady Michelle smiled. "You deal with the Elected Officials. I will deal with the Lords personally,"

Janet took the beads from Lady Michelle, rushed back home and got to work on the gifts.

Time was running out for her kind.

***

Janet sat in front of her massive TV with her beautiful husband next to her as she watched all the Elected Officials of the UK Government vote on the Anti-Magic Bill.

Her small living room smelt of the lavender, scented oils and oranges that she had used to make all the gifts and now she hoped that her hard work had been enough.

She had made every one of them the best gift she could and Janet just hoped it was enough to make them support magic.

According to the News, this was the first time ever in Parliament's history that every single member had been present to take part in a vote. Normally that would have concerned her, but tonight she couldn't care less.

Janet gripped her husband's magically charged hands tighter as a tall man stood up on the television and read out the results.

Her heart was thumping in her chest as the next few seconds would determine her life, her husband's life and the life of her people.

"The Yeses have 2 Votes. The Noes have 598 Votes. The Noes have it. The Noes have it!"

Janet felt an immense wave of relaxation wash over her, but the sound from the television was deafening as every single (minus the two that voted yes) Elected Official jumped up and celebrated.

No one wanted magic to be outlawed.

And it was all because of Janet. Sure no one would ever know how she had saved magic, but Janet didn't care. She only cared about the making of her gifts, sharing the joy and most importantly showing people how magic binds everyone together in joy.

Whatever tomorrow was going to bring, Janet looked forward to it because she had saved magic, got the contract with Lord Michelle and now she was even helping Lady Michelle sell her gifts internationally as part of her side business.

But all that could wait.

Because tonight Janet was going to celebrate with the man she loved, and there was nothing that was going to stop her as she took him off to the bedroom for a long amazing night.

FANTASTICAL CHRISTMAS VOLUME 1

ONE FINAL CHRISTMAS

The last thing I cared about was what the non-magic doctors were calling my cancer, they thought I had lung, bowel and bone cancer.

But they were wrong.

I couldn't blame them for being wrong, they weren't the specialist magic doctors like they had in certain parts of the world. These doctors in Southeast England were hardly that good at detecting magic.

I doubted they even believed in magic. That only made me feel more sorry for them, magic was an amazing thing to believe in, see and even touch it.

I hated the pain that shot through my bones every few seconds as the magical cancer pulsed through me towards my heart and brain. The cancer was going to kill me, I knew that for sure.

But as I turned on my soft cold hospice bed to look outside, I could only wish that I could pass through the window and go into that beautiful white snow.

The snow was falling quickly in massive flakes and on Christmas Day morning, the entire Southeast would wake up to a blanket of snow. It would definitely be a white Christmas.

That made me feel amazing.

I had always used my magic to make others happy. Poor children got rich, a dysfunctional family suddenly found a solution and the unfortunate became fortunate. All I had ever wanted to do was make others happy.

The smell of harsh chemicals mixed with the awful hints of urine made my stomach turn as my mouth filled with the taste of chemical lemons and I remembered how badly I wanted the cancer to take me. I was more than happy for the hospice to take me but I didn't realise everywhere would stink of urine, poo and chemicals.

A shot of pain pulsed up my spine and settled at the top, I didn't need to be told to know that the cancer was preparing to shoot into my brain and kill me.

The sound of the wind howling outside was like a siren call to me and I wanted, needed to go outside. But I was too weak from the cancer.

Why did I have to try and make a cursed family happy?

That's how you get magic cancer apparently. I was just walking along a long street at the time, saw a family frowning and decided I wanted to make their day. That was last Christmas. I cast a spell, it backfired horribly and pure dark energy shot into me.

That's when I realise the family had to be cursed by one of my magical brothers or sisters for something the family had done. If I had known then I would have left them, but I didn't. I tried to do the right thing and now I was dying.

I had even tried to reach out to my magical brothers and sisters and even magical parents, but they didn't listen to me. They probably thought I was trying to break magical law by trying to help out a cursed family. I couldn't blame them.

The sound of little paws tapping on the floor made me get up, bite down my agony and a wave of excitement filled me when I saw a ghost cat.

The cat was just as beautiful as I remembered with its long purple, blue and pink fur and its loud purring filling the room.

"My Familiar," I whispered as it stroked its cold ghostly fur.

My stomach relaxed as I stroked my Familiar again, it was great to see my oldest friend. The little cat had died years ago from old age, leaving me alone to bring joy to the world and Christmas cheer to all the good children.

I wished Familiar had been alive last Christmas, she would have known the family was cursed and stopped me. She would have saved me before I did what I always did, act first, think later.

Familiar brushed against my legs and I felt something. I felt as if she was urging me to follow her outside.

My heart skipped a few beats as I remembered something in magical law about the return of your Familiar and your death.

"It's time, isn't it?" I asked.

Familiar nodded and whipped her tail against the floor.

I looked outside in the snow. I so badly wanted to go outside, feel the snow a final time and walk over to the other side. But a tiny part of me didn't feel ready.

Then again, what did I have to live for?

I was stuck in some urine, poo and chemical scented hospice with no friends and no one to miss me. At least if I died outside, I would get to die on my own terms and once again be permanently reunited with my magical brothers and sisters.

"Come on then Familiar," I said, getting up.

I grabbed my awfully thin robe, old slippers and my ancient magical cap. At least the cap would allow me to die looking good, the only magic it had was the ability to make the wearer look stunning.

If I was going to die, I wasn't going to look like every other old fart in this place!

Familiar bounced outside my door and meowed for me to hurry up.

I went outside my room. I had always hated the cold sterile white of these long hallways, there was no love, respect or compassion here. The entire hospice was waiting for us to die so they could get rid of us and collect more money from the government.

Familiar meowed again. She bounced along the hallway towards the exit at the very end.

I shuffled along.

This was ridiculous. Last Christmas I would easily run down the hallway and be out of here within a minute, now I didn't know. I was so slow, I was so pointless, maybe my death would be a good thing.

I kept shuffling and Familiar bounced down towards me and bit me.

The pain didn't feel bad and Familiar injected me with some of her own blood, the pain felt nice.

Anything was better than the agony that kept pulsing up my spine as the magical cancer prepared for the final blow.

As mine and Familiar's blood mixed I felt a surge of power, energy and love fill me. I walked normally up the hallway but I heard Familiar bounce slowly behind me.

I didn't know how much blood she had given me but even ghosts could die in this mortal realm. I couldn't bear the idea of my oldest friend dying on me permanently.

My dream had always been to die and find her again in the afterlife. I dreamed of playing day and night with her like we used to.

But now she had decided I was the most important thing that she had to save.

The two massive wooden doors with two little glass mini-windows ahead of me led to the reception area and the exit. I went to push against them but I looked back at Familiar who was dragging herself over to me.

I dashed over to her, picked her up and pushed against the two massive doors.

They weren't moving.

They were locked.

I felt the magical cancer spiral up my spine slowly.

Familiar hit her head against my arm. She felt so cold, almost icy. But I felt the urge to throw her at the door.

I did.

She didn't even scream.

Then I saw her on the other side of the door and she meowed so loudly that I had to cover my ears. Thank the Magic non-magic humans couldn't hear her.

The two doors unlocked.

I hissed as the magical cancer bit into the base of my neck.

Familiar chomped on my leg.

Again I felt energy, strength and love fill me but I didn't like it. I didn't want Familiar to die. So I picked her up, walked through the reception area missing all the rows upon rows of horrible chairs and tables and pushed the exit door open.

A loud alarm started to go off and I kept walking.

The bitter freezing cold hung onto me as I went down the stone steps and into the snow covered road.

There weren't any cars about and the only sound was the defeating alarm so the sad truth was the hospice staff would be out here soon.

But I didn't care. I loved the amazing cold wind and snow that blow around me, chilling my skin and making my thin useless robe flap in the wind. Even the hints of Christmas spices in the air probably coming from a nearby house only made tonight even more magical.

Because now I could happily die knowing I had experienced one final Christmas with my Familiar out in the wonderful white snow and dying on my own terms.

Familiar gently tapped her head against my chest and I felt the urge to look back at the hospice. I instantly smiled when I saw my body dead on the stairs, surrounded by three hospice staff.

I kissed Familiar's head, savouring her beautiful purple, blue and pink fur because she had proved something to me. She might be weak because she wanted to save me so badly, but she was alive.

And now I was dead, I would take care of her like I always dreamed of, nurse her back to health and then we could play day and night like we both wanted.

Now this really was the perfect Final Christmas.

AUTHOR'S CHRISTMAS PROBLEMS

Even since I was born before The Great War I had always loved Christmas and how it had changed over the decades. I loved all the gift giving, the courting and the grand Christmas parties that use to happen last century, and I seriously enjoy the more modern Christmases too.

I always make sure I do my Christmas shopping early in December so it leaves Christmas Eve and Christmas Day free for me to go out and do my job.

And yes, it is a very fortunate factor that I get to work on Christmas day.

But thankfully Christmas Day was only three days away, and I was seriously looking forward to that.

My name is Matilda Plum, a superhero in the counselling, therapy and psychology sector. It is my job and utter passion to travel round helping people, solve their problems and maintain their mental health.

It's a great job and I love it.

I also love that Christmas time is both my busiest and quietest times of the year as everyone is filled with merriment, happiness and all that sense of goodwill crap that we teach children to believe in.

I was walking down a particularly wonderful stretch of Canterbury high street in England with the delightfully cold air blowing gently just chilling my skin enough to know it was cold, but not too much that I wanted to go home.

There were plenty of little shops with Christmas lights, decorative and free samples of mulled wine (I got so drunk going to all the shops sampling their goods one year). And the sound of people singing carols in the distance made me smile.

There was so much goodwill in the air that I loved it, but I was NOT letting carollers stop me, not when I had a job to do. Because in my opinion, carollers are the plague of Christmas, most of them can't sing, they're too bubbly and they won't go away unless you give them money.

I was just about to take my shopping bags, filled with fresh vegetables, meats and other things I needed for my annual Psychology Superheroes Dinner, into a very large kitchenware store (because my friends broke my roasting tins. Don't ask!) when I sensed something.

You see being a superhero psychologist meant all the myths and misconceptions about psychologists are my superpowers, and right now my spidey sense was telling me not to go in the kitchenware store but to go into the bookstore next door.

I looked at the large four-storey high bookstore for a moment with its tinsel, Christmas lights and Christmas displays in the window for a moment. And I did need to grab my friend Octavia, a superhero in the gambling sector, a book for Christmas.

So I might as well kill two birds with one stone.

As I entered the very large bookstore I was surprised at the sheer amount of little wooden tables in rows in front of me filled with brand new books from so many authors.

Then I noticed how the bookstore had ever so carefully created a pathway for readers to start looking at one genre and end up at the same table. My superhero powers were telling me there were so many little tricks here that made a customer behave like the owners wanted, that it was so clever.

Just not what I was here for.

But I did go over to the large table next to the counter to see what book the owners were trying to push so hard. I was rather underwhelmed, I had been expecting something sensational, maybe a romance, maybe a fantasy book but nope. It was only the latest book by a writer me and millions of customers had gone off.

I sneered at the book and heard the young woman behind the tills laugh quietly. I looked up and her and focused on her long brown hair, tasteful green uniform and long pink nails. She looked great.

"Am I not the only one to do that?" I asked.

The woman carefully moved her head in the direction of a security camera and I understood she didn't want to get into trouble and I understood that.

Since the woman had spoken to me, I used my analysis superpowers to learn that she was a very bright woman from a nearby university who just wanted to finish work on Christmas Eve and go home to her family up in London.

Yet she was concerned about whether or not she would have enough money for petrol.

As much as I don't believe that all humans do actually show the Christmas spirit, I know I always try. So I picked up the awful book on the table, went over to the young woman and subtly gave her a £50 note and bought the damn book too.

The woman subtly smiled and thanked me for the money and I was about to leave when she said something to me.

"You know the author's upstairs you know," she said.

My superpowers urged me to go up and talk to him.

I seriously didn't want to because the entire reason why me and millions of others didn't like his books anymore was because his stories were just so repetitive, the endings were rubbish and the author had turned to drugs.

Personally the whole drug thing doesn't bother me because I know he just needs professional people, but given how bad his books were getting. I didn't have time for bad stories, so I refused to read him now.

Yet I am a superhero first. I had to talk to him.

"Thank you," I said to the woman and I went upstairs taking my rather heavy shopping bags with me.

***

It took me another half an hour until I had finished searching the entire bookstore and found the author in a very dark corner of the bookstore surrounded by horror novels that were on clearance.

The author wasn't very tall, maybe five foot at the very most, he wore dirty blue (I think) jeans, a dirty t-shirt and shoes that must have been bought last century.

This really wasn't how I imagined this author looking.

Even though I was in what I call winter clothes wearing some black jeans, a long thick coat and with my hair dyed green (don't ask!). I still looked far, far better.

As I stood next to him, wanting to be sick at the smell of his cigarettes, weed and the musty books around us. I just wanted to help him, and help make his Christmas a little better.

"Hello?" I asked.

The man didn't even acknowledge who I was, I got out the book I had just bought because I needed to double check what his real name was. He wrote under the name Samuel Ratcliff, but it turned out his real name was Sam Jenkins.

"Sam Jenkins," I said.

Again Sam didn't even react to me.

I slowly started to hum a merry little Christmas tune to myself that was charged with superpowers and as it entered Sam's mind. I began to analyse and learn a lot about him.

Wow.

I knew from the newspapers and local news channels that he had had a rough time of late with drugs, some escorts and other things. But it turned out his wife had filed for divorce for cheating on her, he had spent his life saving on weed and his publisher was about to blacklist him from the industry.

And I knew it shouldn't have come as a surprise to me, but he was seriously starting to consider suicide.

Of course as a superhero I had to stop that, but I also had to somehow improve his life.

"Your wife isn't happy then," I said.

Sam slowly turned to face me. "How do you know? Did my publisher send you? I told them I don't want to write another fantasy mystery book,"

That was what I could use to help him.

"I am… a friend Sam, I was a reader actually,"

"Was?" Sam said.

I knew how upset he was knowing he had lost readers, but his emotion was so raw, painful and he wasn't happy in the slightest.

"I used to love your books. In the 90s they were

my bread and butter, I would run home from secondary school each day and my teenage self would read a new book,"

It was a complete lie considering how old I was, but it seemed to make him smile.

"I just can't go on. I hate writing. I hate my life. Even my own family hates me," Sam said.

And that was my path to helping him, I loved it when my clients (which Sam basically was at this point) basically told me how to help them.

Then Sam started to leave. "It was nice meeting you,"

A dark black aura formed around him, he was about to die.

I grabbed him. "You don't have to do this Sam. You can love your writing again, your fans love you still. Hell, I love you,"

Sam sighed, folded his arms and just looked at me. I knew I had some work to do.

"Please, whoever you are. Just... just let me go. The world will not even notice that I'm gone," Sam said.

I gestured to all the horror books on the shelves.

"People will miss you. Your family will miss you. Your kids will especially. If you do this then there is no coming back," I said calmly.

He really focused on all the books.

"I already," Sam said, "have a legacy. My books will be what people talk about,"

I had to laugh at that. Not very professional I

know, but I felt like it would prove a point.

And I seriously had to put down these shopping bags. I was laughing so much the bags kept shaking.

"What legacy is that Sam? People hate you and your books, but it doesn't have to be that way,"

Sam pushed away from me and he started to walk towards the stairs.

I focused my influencing superpowers to make him stop. He did.

"Then the world is better without me," Sam said.

I pretended to start crying. "But Sam! We need your stories. Your family loves you,"

Sam slowly started nodding. "I know you're lying about most of this. I don't know who you are but you can't help me,"

Wow! This guy was not making it easy for me.

I quickly searched his mind to see why his publisher kept making him write another fantasy mystery, and to my surprise they weren't. They were making him write whatever he wanted, it was Sam had didn't want to write.

Not the publisher.

"You really don't want to do writing anymore, do you?" I asked.

Sam nodded. "It's boring, lonely and awful. I want to be with my kids but the rewriting as much as I love it, takes so long,"

Well, I was really starting to feel like I couldn't save him, so I picked my heavy shopping bags up.

From what I understand about Sam Jenkins was

a man who lived for his writing, family and probably the so-called privilege that came from being a writer. He didn't want to write anymore, his family didn't like him and he clearly had no privilege left.

So I was going to have to make him do something for me. And it wasn't fun trying to hold some large shopping bags.

Making my superpowers as strong as I possibly could I sent into the deepest, darkest corners of his mind to and see his wife and take me with him.

Sam shook his head a few times then he hissed and looked at me.

"Actually, if you really think I can be saved. Come home with me, meet my wife and know how terrible of a situation I'm in?"

I pretended to act like I might be crossing a line.

"Please," Sam said.

Even I was surprised at the emotional pain in his voice. He really was at the end of his tether and I seriously didn't trust him to drive us home.

So I grabbed him and we teleported off.

I just needed to drop off my shopping bags first.

***

One of the best things about a superhero is when we teleport the world becomes blurry to people for a millisecond then it's like we were always there. People aren't surprised or don't even suspect we weren't there a second ago.

Sam thought the same thing.

He knocked on his front door, his wife frowned

as we entered and she led us into a very modern kitchen. It was rather lovely actually with its bright copper tones, kitchen island and red and green tinsel hanging from the lights.

Then the little tunes of Christmas playing softly in the background.

"What do you want? You stink of weed," the wife said.

As the two spoke (loudly) I tapped into my analysis superpowers and the wife only confirmed what I already knew. She really did love him, he was the centre of her entire universe and she hated doing this. But as she saw it she had to do what was in the best interest of their children and herself.

Then to edge things along, I implanted the suggestion of Sam getting on his knees and being truly vulnerable with his wife. Something he had never done before, and something she really wanted.

Sam did it immediately.

"Bertice, I love you more than anything else in the world," Sam said.

As Sam continued explaining himself, how he didn't want to be a writer anymore, how he felt so disappointed into himself and more. I had to admit Bertice was an awful name.

After a few moments Bertice knelt down on the ground to, they both kissed, said they would work things out and then she asked him how many roast potatoes he wanted on the big day.

After a quick cup of coffee, Sam showed me on

the way out and as me and him stood outside of their house, he asked me a question I didn't know how to answer.

"I don't know what you did, but thank you. I mean it. But who are you?"

"You're welcome," I said and gently kissed him on the cheek. "Happy Christmas,"

Then I teleported away and landed back in my very large, expensive bedroom and I just collapsed on my soft sheets.

I didn't know how to answer that question because I was so many things. A psychologist, a superhero, a saver and the rest. I did so much but I was always the person who was going to help the innocent, solve their problems and protect their mental health.

And whilst Sam might never write again, at least I saved him, and you never know he might write something, maybe something better than before and I really, really hope so.

But my friend Octavia was definitely getting that book I bought. I wasn't reading it, I wanted something new, exciting and different.

And I had a strange Christmas feeling that I wouldn't have to wait too long. Not long at all.

LAST WINTER DRAGON EGG

Immortals die. You just need the right weapon.

Guardian Genesis Oakley stood at attention like she always did in her massive orange cave that rose so high into the sky that she was always interested in how much it was from the ground.

She never knew what happened above the ground too much these days. She knew who was in power, did they know about magic and the rest, but if someone asked her what the singers, celebrities or footballers of the world were. Then she would be useless.

Genesis utterly loved her cave with its massive feeling and appearance. She once timed herself actually running as fast as she could (which probably broke an Olympic record or two) and it still took her an hour to get from one side of her cave to another. So it would probably take a normal person four hours to run from one side to another.

Her cave was massive!

Genesis loved how the bright glowing crystals that grew out of the cave's domed ceiling illumined the cave with such natural intensity that Genesis never had to readjust her eyes when she went outside.

And combine that with the wonderful sound and refreshing taste of the natural spring water that flowed down the very, very end of the cave, it was simply the best place to live whilst she completed her duty.

Genesis always stood at attention in front of a very large pillar of solid granite with a single snowy white egg on top. It was easily twice the size of a normal human baby, and it contained one of the most precious things in the entire world.

A winter dragon.

Of all the dragons from the Chinese to fire-breathing to the Nature dragons and all the hundreds of different types in-between. Genesis had to admit her absolute favourite dragon was the winter one, well at least from the photos she had seen.

Genesis loved its snowy white scales, large pointy head like a snowplough and massive wings that were perfect for flapping away the snow. They were the perfect dragon for winter and that's why they were so loved and valued in Scotland, Iceland and Scandinavia.

Yet when the English invaded the Scots back in 1296, it didn't take them long to find the peacefully sleeping Winter dragons and a bunch of others that weren't a threat. But the English just killed them and then drank the dragon blood as a reward.

Genesis still laughed at that last part. Dragon blood was extremely poisonous to killers, if an innocent person drank it then it would cure them. But that was never going to happen to the English soldiers that slaughtered Scotland that year and every year since.

Genesis had been watching the Winter Dragons at the time, and laughing with her Scottish friends about the rumours of an English invasion. No one had wanted to believe the English would invade their neighbour just because they signed The Auld Alliance.

But they did.

As soon as Genesis saw the English coming, she grabbed a couple of dragon eggs (it was all she could carry) and ran as far as she could. She eventually found the wonderful cave she was in and now she was just waiting.

Waiting for the very last winter dragon to be born.

Genesis had watched the other egg she had carried away hatch hundreds of years ago but that dragon was ill, deformed and twisted.

It had died within ten years of life, but there was a reason why that still shocked Genesis to this very day. The dragon had transferred its life force to Genesis to make her immortal, so she could always watch over and protect the dragons.

Yet Genesis just knew that with the right weapon even immortals could and would die.

If anything else, her own immortality was a tiny piece of comfort compared to the only other gift that poor lovely dragon had given her.

For when she needed it most, Genesis would shoot fire out of her hands and form a flaming sword, and Genesis really hoped she had the power to summon other dragons but she wasn't sure.

She really wasn't sure on that part.

Genesis focused on the delightful warmth of the dragon egg in front of her as she watched it for a few more moments. She couldn't help but feel like something awful was about to happen, but she just had to focus on the egg in case she died.

Before the Winter Dragons were slaughtered, Genesis heard one of them mutter a prophecy that she really knew would come true throughout the centuries.

It was a rather simple prophecy for a dragon (Genesis realised centuries ago how complex some were!). It simply stated that one day, one winter, one moment near Christmas, an Englishman would come for the egg. If he won and took the egg, then dragons would become extinct within a hundred years and humanity would die too. If not, the dragons would never die and no humans would ever be hurt.

Genesis had always hated people who hunted and killed dragons. Thankfully so few people knew about dragons anymore, so very, very few people hunted them.

Yet Genesis had heard whispers of a group

getting more and more powerful and they were slowly (thankfully extremely slowly) revealing to the world the existence of dragons. And trying to convince them of them being dangerous.

Genesis just wanted to laugh at them. Dragons were no more dangerous than your domestic dog and cat.

The sound of cold heavy footsteps echoed throughout the entire cave and Genesis turned around.

Genesis kept a perfectly straight face as she focused on the terribly handsome man that stood ten metres from her. She just knew he had to possess some kind of supernatural speed to be able to travel that quickly from her secret staircase on the other side of the cave to where she was now.

The man was surprisingly handsome with his smooth middle-aged face, brown hair and tight fitting knights armour.

That little detail seriously surprised her, but considering she was wearing what could only be described as Jedi robes. She supposed she couldn't judge too harshly.

Genesis clocked the two large longswords in his hands and there was such a hungry in his eyes. This man just wanted to kill her and get the dragon egg.

The prophecy never went on to mention what the English did with the dragon egg if she failed. In fact, it only said that an Englishman would take it, it didn't say if the Englishman was working for the

English or someone else.

But Genesis had to stop him no matter what.

Genesis was about to say something to the man when she noticed something she couldn't quite understand. It was something in those cold dark eyes of his, she had seen them before.

Yes.

Genesis recognised those eyes from almost 800 years ago, she would recognise the sheer coldness of those eyes anywhere. Because this was the man who led the English troops to slaughter the dragons all those years ago.

This was the monster who robbed the world of so much beauty and this was the man who deserved to die for all the suffering he had bought her.

As much as Genesis didn't want to admit it, she had wanted to die naturally. She wanted to find love, have kids and live a life full of joy and wonder in Scotland, like all the other young women.

But no. Because this Englishman was such an idiot, fearful monster he had robbed her of all of it.

"You recognise me then traitor," he said coldly.

Genesis didn't even want to give him the respect of talking to him. Sure, she might have been English once, but when the war with the French had gotten to the point of being, well, pointless to some extent, Genesis had fled to Scotland in search of a new life.

That had quickly ended with the Auld Alliance. A rather innocent agreement to make sure that Scotland was always protected from the English, and France was too.

Genesis had met some of the Scottish clan chiefs and King John. They were great people. Sure, there were raids in Northern England but it did not mean an entire country deserved to be slaughtered because of one King's embarrassment.

"The egg will look nice over some toast," he said.

Genesis flicked out her wrists. Two flaming swords shot out.

"I will not allow you to do that. This is an innocent creature. Not that the English has ever cared about that," Genesis said.

The Englishman laughed. "What is such a *wee* woman like yourself gonna do?"

Genesis charged forward.

Jumping into the air.

The Englishman whipped out his swords.

He swung.

Genesis blocked them.

He kicked her.

Genesis stumbled.

The man shot forward.

Swinging his swords.

Genesis tried to block.

She failed.

The swords sliced her cheek.

Genesis flew at him.

Her swords flaming.

Sparks rained down on the cave.

The man hissed.

The sparks were engulfing him.

His skin burned.

Genesis kept swinging.

The man kept blocking.

The man jumped forward.

Knocking Genesis to the ground.

The man rammed his sword into her hands.

Genesis's flaming swords disappeared.

As Genesis screamed in crippling pain as she stared her hands with two swords rammed through them.

She couldn't move. She couldn't fight. She couldn't do anything.

Genesis wanted to do something but she was trapped. She was unable to do anything except hurt herself.

Genesis focused on shooting flames out of her hands. Yet she was in too much pain.

The Englishman laughed so loud that it harshly echoed around the entire cave and he went over to the dragon eggs.

Taking out a knife.

Genesis screamed in horror.

Blue flames shot out of her hands.

The swords glowed bright red.

Then white.

They melted.

Genesis laughed in delight as the swords melted around her but they didn't burn her. They formed themselves in two daggers for her.

Genesis grabbed them.

She charged.

The man spun around.

Whipping out a pistol.

He shot.

The bullet ripped through Genesis's stomach.

She slammed onto the cold ground.

Genesis tried to cope with the immense pain that filled her chest, stomach and soul as she felt her blood slowly gush out of her.

She hated this Englishman more than anything else in the world. All she wanted to do was protect this dragon egg so another life could be spared from this senseless violence.

That was never going to happen. Genesis knew that now.

She even felt her immortality and the remaining magic in her crackle away as Genesis realised that she wasn't shot with a normal bullet.

Genesis was going to die today.

"What do the Scottish bitches have on their toast?" the man asked. "Oh wait toast is probably too sophisticated for the barbarians,"

Almost 800 years had passed, the English no more respected Scotland now then they had all those years ago. Genesis hated that fact, she had travelled down to England two decades ago as she wanted to check in on the other dragon populations.

Yet she quickly returned to her cave and hurried back from London. The people there saw her as some kind of strange alien being that didn't deserve to be in *their* United Kingdom.

Genesis so badly wanted that to change one day.

Genesis felt the man stand over her. Pressing a blade against her throat.

"This is for all the Scots that my stupid country left alive that day," the man said.

Genesis wanted to point out there wasn't that many left. But it was a pointless comment. Then she heard something crack.

"How are you still alive?" Genesis asked, really playing up her Scottish accent.

More cracking echoed around the cave.

The man smiled. "If you torture enough dragons. One of them is bound to give you something,"

Genesis's eyes widened in horror.

The man raised the knife. He was going to end Genesis.

A white blur jumped on the man's back. It screamed. It roared. It chomped.

Blood splashed on Genesis's face.

The man screamed in agony as chunks were ripped from his back.

His head cracked.

Blood, muscle and brain matter painting the walls of the cave.

When the man's foul corpse slammed onto the cave floor, Genesis smiled when a very small, no bigger than a human child, snowy white dragon jumped onto her chest.

Genesis almost couldn't believe how beautiful it was, and because she had tried to buy the dragon as much time as possible. She had managed to keep it safe and buy it time to hatch.

The cute little dragon smelt so refreshing, piney and earthy as it raised one of its little claws and lovingly stroked Genesis's face.

But using the last remains of her strength, Genesis forced herself to lower the little dragon's paws. She knew exactly what it was doing, it was going to save her and sacrifice some of its life force to heal her.

She didn't want it.

For her mission was done. Her duty for the past 800 years had been to protect the dragons and make sure the last winter dragon egg hatched.

And now she had done it.

The little snowy white dragon kissed her and slowly nodded. Genesis was more than glad the amazing little dragon seemed to understand and immense coldness coated Genesis as the last of her life drained away from her.

Yet not before she saw the little dragon fly safely away so it could find a dragon pack and be loved and treasured and protected.

Genesis had done her job and now she could die happily and very, very proud.

SACRIFICE FOR SATURNALIA

Kneeling on the cold soft mud surrounded by beautiful oak trees and bushes, I always have had a soft spot for English woodland. But I have to say that whilst I am far from a pagan, religious or anything to do with superstition. I love Saturnalia. I flat love it.

I love how the festival back in ancient roman turned society on its head by allowing a bit of chaos to spread. It's amazing how gambling, Masters serving slaves and other wonderous things were allowed on Saturnalia, but forbidden at all other times of the year.

That's why I love it. It was the one time of the night where the world could fall to chaos and everyone would celebrate it.

So when me and my witch and wizard friends mentioned recreating a Saturnalia for ourselves, who was I to say no?

Of course we weren't going to do the more religious side of the festival, but we were definitely going to take part in the gaff gift giving part. That was going to be amazing. I had already got all my friends a light up Santa who said rude things to them, that was perfect for my friends.

The cold howl of the wind chilled me as my knees sank further into the freezing mud as there was a small path in front of me in this woodland, where I was hoping that a small rabbit or something would cross so I could catch it for the Saturnalia.

The others might have said we didn't need a sacrifice to open the festival but I completely disagree. The sacrifice was the thing that kicked off the amazing feasts, gambling and the rest of the night. I had to have a sacrifice.

The smell of the cold air was filled with hints of damp, pine and sweet flowers as I peeked through the bushes to see if anything was coming along the path.

A lot of people might have believed (rightly) that this was a lot of trouble to go to for a silly outdated festival, but as much as I love Christmas with all the presents, food and family things. I suppose in a way Christmas is rather outdated considering we now know that Jesus was actually born in June and his birth was moved to combine with Saturnalia.

Leading to the creation of Christmas.

So this might be a lot of horrible effort for a festival, but I did want to impress someone special to me.

One of the young witches I know, Sandra, is stunning with her long golden hair, bright blue eyes and her wonderful body. She's amazing! Especially when it comes to her magic, she can do things I can't even imagine.

Anyway, she'll be there and I want to impress her. I want her to take notice of me. I want her to… maybe even talk to me.

It sounds silly but I really, really want her to like me.

A shriek echoed around the woodland.

I felt something sharp dig into the back of me.

I looked at the thing digging into me to see it was a knife and there was a tall woman pointing it at me. I tried to see what she was like but she was wearing an ugly large black cover and mask that covered all of her face except her bright blue eyes.

"What are you doing here?" the woman said firmly.

I recognised that voice. It was smooth, angelic and beautiful. I was glad it belonged to Sandra, but why the hell would she be here? She was meant to be cooking with the others.

"Sandra?" I asked.

The young beautiful witch took off her mask without even touching it, revealing her smooth stunning face that I wanted to kiss so badly.

"What are *you* doing here?" I asked.

Sandra frowned. "*I* wanted some herbs for a potion tonight. *You* aren't meant to be here,"

"I just wanted to get us a sacrifice tonight,"

Sandra rolled her eyes.

Great! Now she hated me. She wasn't going to

respect me, become friends with me and maybe in the far distance future fall in love with me. She was never going to be that!

A bird fell out of the sky.

Me and Sandra went out onto the path to have a closer look, but we both gasped. This wasn't a bird. It was a bleeding phoenix that was slowly turning to ash.

Sandra let her out her glowing blue magic and started to do something to it, but I could only stand there. The Phoenix was so beautiful with its shiny feathers. It didn't deserve to die.

"Damn it," Sandra said.

All the Phoenix turned to ash.

"It's okay. It will come back in a few minutes," I said.

Sandra shook her head. "Don't be silly. That's only if the ashes aren't scattered in those minutes,"

The wind started to blow.

Me and Sandra wrapped our arms around the ashes.

"Who could attack such a beautiful creature?" I asked.

"What makes you think it was a person?" Sandra asked.

"There was a perfect hole in the Phoenix. Nature isn't that perfect,"

I heard a rustle in the bushes and saw a shadow dash through the trees.

I was really starting to think that we weren't alone out here and I feared that we were going to be the sacrifice for someone else's Saturnalia, whether we liked it or not.

An arrow flew past my head.

Slamming into a tree.

Another flew past.

Catching my ear.

I jumped to one side.

Sandra hissed.

The wind flew.

Blowing the ashes away.

Sandra jumped up.

Someone whacked her over the head.

I looked up to see who had attacked her, only to see a fat horribly overweight man that smelt of sweat, urine and poo. I wasn't a fan of the massive crossbow in his hands. But what troubled me more was the humming like a choir of magical energy that radiated from the arrows.

"She'd make a fine sacrifice, don't ya think boy?"

For starters I'm 23 years old, and this foul bestial man was not having my Sandra!

I thrusted out my hand.

Only a few sparks shot out.

The man laughed. "Seriously? Are you even allowed to call yourself a wizard or warlock?"

I wasn't going to answer that.

"No matter boy. I'll take her, gut her and sacrifice her to the Glory of Saturn,"

Oh great of all the people to find out here tonight, I just had to find myself a hardcore pagan.

Normally pagans are wonderful people, I know tons of them, but this one seemed to be an extremist. Not fun!

"You won't take her!" I shouted.

The man clicked his fingers.

A sharp burning sensation shot up me.

"Saturn rewards me for my service. Me and my friends work each day to honour his Will. He ruled over the Earth once, he shall do it once more,"

Oh great. Not only was this man an extremist, he was a nutter too!

The man pointed the unloaded crossbow at me like he was trying to make a hard decision.

"Now the question is boy. Do I take you both as a better offering to Glorious Saturn?"

As much as I didn't want to answer, this felt like one of those times where whatever you say might be better than silence.

"I doubt it. Saturn will be getting a lot of sacrifices tonight. You can't overfeed him. Think of Saturn getting indigestion. If I was him I would be furious at the person who overfed me,"

The man clicked his fingers again.

I screamed.

"You! Dare to think what Glorious Saturn is thinking,"

He clicked his fingers again and again.

I screamed in agony.

"No," I muttered, as I saw one of Sandra's fingers twitch.

If I could just buy her a bit more time then I might be able to give her time to recover and attack. She was the more powerful one after all.

I held out my hand perfectly flat and willed a dancing flame to appear. It did. Only for a second or two.

The man laughed. "Ya pathetic boy. You couldn't even save a fly if your life depended on it,"

He was right. He was so right, I was worthless as far as magic was concerned. I had failed all my magic classes at school and if anything bad was to happen, I might as well have been a paper bag against a tsunami.

But I wasn't useless at everything.

"You know Mighty Chosen of Saturn, it might please Glorious Saturn if you teach me some magic,"

The man spat at me.

"Isn't the spirit of Saturnalia meant to be filling the world with a bit of chaos and turning the social order on its head?"

The man grunted and nodded. "Fine boy. The key to magic is just letting the Will flow through ya. Magic isn't ya enemy. It's a force. Don't resist,"

I willed the dancing flame to appear again. A bright blue, green and yellow flame danced against the wind for seconds before I stopped it.

I couldn't help but smile. "Wow, thank you!"

The man laughed and he had a strange look in his eyes. It was partly haunted, partly happy. As if he had taught other young people how to use magic before and loved teaching, then it was ripped away from him for some reason.

"Is your family celebrating Saturnalia with you?" I asked.

The man's smile disappeared. "No. My family... my family..."

I frowned and put my hands up in some sort of apology.

"I'm sorry. I didn't mean to bring it up,"

The man frowned. His eyes narrowed. He clicked four times.

Crippling pain filled me.

I fell on my back.

I clutched my stomach.

The man rushed over.

He stomped on my stomach.

Again and again.

Sandra shot up.

Thrusting out her hand.

Magic energy shot out.

Slamming into the man.

It exploded against him.

The air hummed with magical energy.

The man whipped out his crossbow.

He fired.

I jumped up.

Shooting out my hand.

I willed the arrows to stop.

They melted.

Sandra thrusted out her other hand.

Even more energy slammed into the man.

He screamed.

The energy turned to fire.

The man screamed as his body charred, smouldered and turned to ash.

When Sandra lowered her hands, she looked at me and smiled. In the years I had known her, she had never ever looked at me. And right now, she was. She was giving me a massive smile.

"You did well I guess," she said, something in her voice making it sound playful.

The pile of ashes were blown away in the wind and I couldn't help but feel sad for the man in a way. He must have lost his family, fallen into depression and found an Extremist Pagan group as support. It was a shame he didn't have someone to support him, something I never wanted my friends to have.

And that was the true reason I loved Saturnalia. Yes there was all the social order turning and the chaos of it, but it was really just an excuse for a celebration to spend time with friends, family and those you would never celebrate with normally (like the Masters and the Slaves of ancient Rome).

But this man and his friends had forgotten that. They shouldn't have wanted to kill anyone tonight, they should have wanted to celebrate with them and enjoy their company.

As I stared at stunning Sandra who still looked even more beautiful despite being whacked over the head with a crossbow, I realised that that was exactly what I wanted to do.

I didn't care about getting a sacrifice for Saturnalia, I just wanted, needed to go and see my friends and celebrate with them. And in a way I suppose I did have a sacrifice for Saturnalia after all, maybe Saturn would enjoy feasting on the man's soul or whatever he feasted on.

So at least the man did get his wish to meet Glorious Saturn wherever he may be.

Sandra started to walk away along the woodland back to the town and back to our friends, but she stopped and held out her hand to me. I didn't know if she was going to shoot fire or magical energy at me.

Yet I took it and she held my hand tight.

I didn't know nor care why, I just enjoyed it and looked forward to where tonight was going to lead us, but I hoped whatever Sandra's interest in me was, it was going to last for a long, long time.

GET YOUR FREE AND EXCLUSIVE SHORT STORY NOW! LEARN ABOUT NEMESIO'S PAST!

https://www.subscribepage.com/fireheart

FANTASTICAL CHRISTMAS VOLUME 1

About the author:

Connor Whiteley is the author of over 60 books in the sci-fi fantasy, nonfiction psychology and books for writer's genre and he is a Human Branding Speaker and Consultant.

He is a passionate warhammer 40,000 reader, psychology student and author.

Who narrates his own audiobooks and he hosts The Psychology World Podcast.

All whilst studying Psychology at the University of Kent, England.

Also, he was a former Explorer Scout where he gave a speech to the Maltese President in August 2018 and he attended Prince Charles' 70th Birthday Party at Buckingham Palace in May 2018.

Plus, he is a self-confessed coffee lover!

More From The Holiday Extravaganza:

Criminal Christmas:
Crime, Christmas, Closet
Protecting Christmas
Christmas Thief
Christmas, Crime, letter
Private Eye, Convention and Christmas
Cheater At Dinner
Perfect Christmas
Salvation In The Maid
Criminal, Resistance, Alliance
Dark Farm
Great Give Away

Sweet Christmas
Lights, Love, Christmas
Journalist, Zookeeper, Love
Young Romantic Hearts
Love In The Newspaper
Holiday, Burnout, Love
Homeless, Charity, Love
Cold December Night
Driving Home For Love
Love At The Winter Wedding
Fireworks, New Year, Love
Loving In The New Year Tourist

Fantastical Christmas:
Magic That Binds
One Final Christmas
Author's Christmas Problems
Last Winter Dragon Egg
A Sacrifice For Saturnalia
Soulcaster
Weird First Christmas
All Feast
Solstice Guardian
Wheel of Years
Repent

OTHER SHORT STORIES BY CONNOR WHITELEY

<u>Mystery Short Stories:</u>
Poison In The Candy Cane
Christmas Innocence
You Better Watch Out
Christmas Theft
Trouble In Christmas
Smell of The Lake
Problem In A Car
Theft, Past and Team
Embezzler In The Room
A Strange Way To Go
A Horrible Way To Go
Ann Awful Way To Go
An Old Way To Go
A Fishy Way To Go
A Pointy Way To Go
A High Way To Go
A Fiery Way To Go
A Glassy Way To Go
A Chocolatey Way To Go
Kendra Detective Mystery Collection Volume 1
Kendra Detective Mystery Collection Volume 2
Stealing A Chance At Freedom

Glassblowing and Death
Theft of Independence
Cookie Thief
Marble Thief
Book Thief
Art Thief
Mated At The Morgue
The Big Five Whoopee Moments
Stealing An Election
Mystery Short Story Collection Volume 1
Mystery Short Story Collection Volume 2

Science Fiction Short Stories:
The First Rememberer
Life of A Rememberer
System of Wonder
Lifesaver
Remarkable Way She Died
The Interrogation of Annabella Stormic
Blade of The Emperor
Arbiter's Truth
Computation of Battle
Old One's Wrath
Puppets and Masters
Ship of Plague
Interrogation
Edge of Failure

One Way Choice
Acceptable Losses
Balance of Power
Good Idea At The Time
Escape Plan
Escape In The Hesitation
Inspiration In Need
Singing Warriors
Knowledge is Power
Killer of Polluters
Climate of Death
The Family Mailing Affair
Defining Criminality
The Martian Affair
A Cheating Affair
The Little Café Affair
Mountain of Death
Prisoner's Fight
Claws of Death
Bitter Air
Honey Hunt
Blade On A Train

Fantasy Short Stories:
City of Snow
City of Light
City of Vengeance
Dragons, Goats and Kingdom
Smog The Pathetic Dragon
Don't Go In The Shed
The Tomato Saver
The Remarkable Way She Died
The Bloodied Rose
Asmodia's Wrath
Heart of A Killer
Emissary of Blood
Dragon Coins
Dragon Tea
Dragon Rider
Sacrifice of the Soul
Heart of The Flesheater
Heart of The Regent
Heart of The Standing
Feline of The Lost
Heart of The Story
City of Fire
Awaiting Death

Other books by Connor Whiteley:

Bettie English Private Eye Series

A Very Private Woman

The Russian Case

A Very Urgent Matter

A Case Most Personal

Trains, Scots and Private Eyes

The Federation Protects

The Fireheart Fantasy Series

Heart of Fire

Heart of Lies

Heart of Prophecy

Heart of Bones

Heart of Fate

City of Assassins (Urban Fantasy)

City of Death

City of Martyrs

City of Pleasure

City of Power

Agents of The Emperor

Return of The Ancient Ones

Vigilance

Angels of Fire

Kingmaker

The Garro Series- Fantasy/Sci-fi
GARRO: GALAXY'S END
GARRO: RISE OF THE ORDER
GARRO: END TIMES
GARRO: SHORT STORIES
GARRO: COLLECTION
GARRO: HERESY
GARRO: FAITHLESS
GARRO: DESTROYER OF WORLDS
GARRO: COLLECTIONS BOOK 4-6
GARRO: MISTRESS OF BLOOD
GARRO: BEACON OF HOPE
GARRO: END OF DAYS

Winter Series- Fantasy Trilogy Books
WINTER'S COMING
WINTER'S HUNT
WINTER'S REVENGE
WINTER'S DISSENSION

Miscellaneous:
RETURN
FREEDOM
SALVATION
Reflection of Mount Flame
The Masked One
The Great Deer

www.ingramcontent.com/pod-product-compliance
Lightning Source LLC
LaVergne TN
LVHW011857060526
838200LV00054B/4384